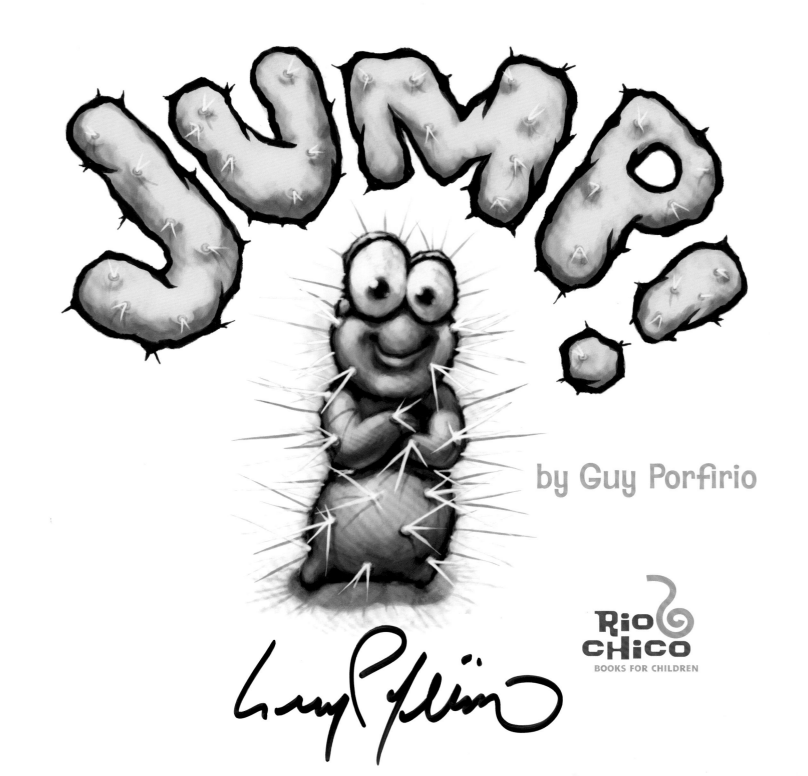

by Guy Porfirio

RIO CHICO
BOOKS FOR CHILDREN

Ordinarily, things were pretty quiet in the desert. But this was no ordinary morning. And Barb was no ordinary cactus.

Barb, you see, wanted an adventure. But, in the desert, nothing ever happened, and nothing ever changed.

Until...

One bright and sunny day, just like all the rest, Ol' Tucker Coyote came a little too close on his way up the path.

Barb saw an opportunity. She held her breath, and waited. At just the right moment, she jumped!

They were off like a shot! Tucker had never moved so fast...ever! Barb stuck on for dear life. Tucker ran in circles, jumped in the air, and rolled on the ground. Then, he ran straight for a rocky cliff—and stopped.

Barb kept going and never looked back.

Fortunately there was a nice, soft place to land.

Before long, she jumped again. Only this time, she flew higher, harder, farther, and faster than ever. The spirit of adventure had really taken hold of her.

Down below, a mighty river raged. Barb dropped
in on a group of river rafters floating along in a giant
inflatable raft. It was quite a leap, even for her.

Suddenly, there was a loud **POP!**

And before she knew it, Barb was riding on the
luggage rack.

Barb coasted down Main Street.

And got a little carried away at the museum of art.

Barb was having the time of her life!

Just when she thought she had seen it all,
she spotted the ocean. Barb had never seen so
much water in her life! She hopped right in.

She jumped with the dolphins, slipped through the seaweed, and bobbed through the bubbles.

The more she jumped, the more she saw.
And the more she saw, the more she jumped.
The world was a marvelous place and it was
getting better by leaps and bounds.

It was smack dab in the middle of Barb's big movie
debut that a terrible ache began to grow in her heart.
"What good is having such a great adventure if there
is no one to share it with?" she thought.
And just like that, an idea jumped right into her head.

Barb jumped onto the very next cowboy home.

Her friends were captivated by her stories of adventure about how she jumped, and she flew, and she swam, and she hopped.

But the best part was when Barb unveiled
her idea—the Coyote Catapult—the first
ever adventure ride for cacti!
Even Tucker was happy about his new job.

Barb's idea took off in no time. The skies became filled with cacti. Her friends appeared in the most peculiar places! **By the dozens!**

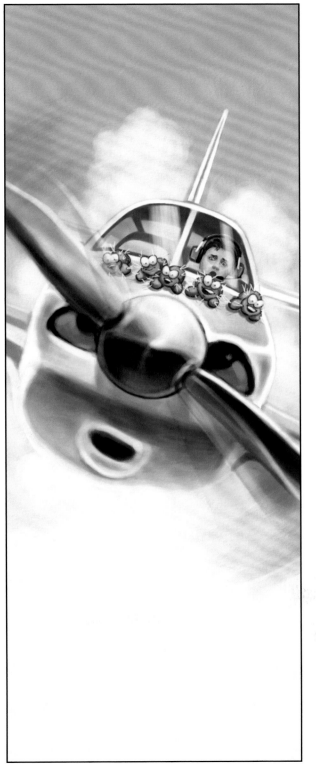

Things weren't exactly ordinary anymore—
and certainly not quiet. Not by a long shot,
which, of course, is just the way Barb liked it.

For Gabriela

Rio Chico, an imprint of Rio Nuevo Publishers®
P. O. Box 5250
Tucson, AZ 85703-0250
(520) 623-9558,
www.rionuevo.com

Editorial: Theresa Howell
Book design: David Jenney

Printed in China.

11   10   9   8   7   17   18   19   20   21

Library of Congress Cataloging-in-Publication Data

Porfirio, Guy.
Jump! / by Guy Porfirio.
    p. cm.
Summary: A little cactus named Barb, yearning for adventure,
jumps on a coyote and from there travels across the desert, to a
city, and even to the ocean before heading home to share the fun
with her friends.
ISBN-13: 978-1-933855-81-3 (hardcover : alk. paper)
ISBN-10: 1-933855-81-9 (hardcover : alk. paper)
[1. Adventure and adventurers—Fiction. 2. Cactus—Fiction.] I.
Title.
PZ7.P7992Jum 2012
[E]—dc23
                        2012001078